Our Silly Garden

by Karen Berman Nagel
Illustrated by Brian Schatell

Hello Reader! — Level 1

SCHOLASTIC INC.
Cartwheel BOOKS®
New York Toronto London Auckland Sydney
Mexico City New Delhi Hong Kong

Today we took some breadcrumbs.
We put them in the ground.

Hello, Family Members,

Learning to read is one of the most important accomplishments of early childhood. **Hello Reader!** books are designed to help children become skilled readers who like to read. Beginning readers learn to read by remembering frequently used words like "the," "is," and "and"; by using phonics skills to decode new words; and by interpreting picture and text clues. These books provide both the stories children enjoy and the structure they need to read fluently and independently. Here are suggestions for helping your child *before, during,* and *after* reading:

Before
- Look at the cover and pictures and have your child predict what the story is about.
- Read the story to your child.
- Encourage your child to chime in with familiar words and phrases.
- Echo read with your child by reading a line first and having your child read it after you do.

During
- Have your child think about a word he or she does not recognize right away. Provide hints such as "Let's see if we know the sounds" and "Have we read other words like this one?"
- Encourage your child to use phonics skills to sound out new words.
- Provide the word for your child when more assistance is needed so that he or she does not struggle and the experience of reading with you is a positive one.
- Encourage your child to have fun by reading with a lot of expression . . . like an actor!

After
- Have your child keep lists of interesting and favorite words.
- Encourage your child to read the books over and over again. Have him or her read to brothers, sisters, grandparents, and even teddy bears. Repeated readings develop confidence in young readers.
- Talk about the stories. Ask and answer questions. Share ideas about the funniest and most interesting characters and events in the stories.

I do hope that you and your child enjoy this book.

—Francie Alexander
  Reading Specialist,
  Scholastic's Learning Ventures

To Ceil S. Berman
A mother who always believes in
all my ideas (silly and otherwise).
—K.B.N.

To Mom
       —B.S.

Text copyright © 2001 by Karen Berman Nagel.
Illustrations copyright © 2001 by Brian Schatell.
All rights reserved. Published by Scholastic Inc.
SCHOLASTIC, HELLO READER, CARTWHEEL BOOKS and associated logos
are trademarks and/or registered trademarks of Scholastic Inc.

ISBN: 0-439-20059-8

Library of Congress Cataloging-in-Publication Data available

12 11 10 9 8 7 6 5 4 3   01 02 03 04 05

Printed in the U.S.A.   24
First printing, March 2001

We sprinkled them with water

and smiled at what we found:

Toast next to the carrots
and toast among the peas!

So we ran to get two pillows,

some socks,

and our dog's fleas.

We also took Mom's hairbrush

and last night's dinner roll.

We buried all our treasure

in one gigantic hole.

Well, the fleas . . .

became . . .

a circus.

But this surprised us most:

The pillows we just planted

were now sheep eating toast!

We tripped over some soccer balls.

They sprang up from the socks.

And we fell into a rocking chair.

It must have grown from rocks.

But then we jumped up in a flash.

The hairbrush had become . . .

a prickly little porcupine,

thanks to our green thumbs!

Will our pennies make a money tree?

Will our piggy bank sprout wings?

Who knows what a garden grows
when you're planting silly things?